Dear Parent:
Your child's love of reading starts here!

Every child learns to read in a different way and at his or her own speed. Some go back and forth between reading levels and read favorite books again and again. Others read through each level in order. You can help your young reader improve and become more confident by encouraging his or her own interests and abilities. From books your child reads with you to the first books he or she reads alone, there are I Can Read Books for every stage of reading:

SHARED READING
Basic language, word repetition, and whimsical illustrations, ideal for sharing with your emergent reader

BEGINNING READING
Short sentences, familiar words, and simple concepts for children eager to read on their own

READING WITH HELP
Engaging stories, longer sentences, and language play for developing readers

READING ALONE
Complex plots, challenging vocabulary, and high-interest topics for the independent reader

ADVANCED READING
Short paragraphs, chapters, and exciting themes for the perfect bridge to chapter books

I Can Read Books have introduced children to the joy of reading since 1957. Featuring award-winning authors and illustrators and a fabulous cast of beloved characters, I Can Read Books set the standard for beginning readers.

A lifetime of discovery begins with the magical words "I Can Read!"

Visit www.icanread.com for information
on enriching your child's reading experience.

ISLAND ADVENTURES

Surf's Up: Island Adventures

™ & © 2007 Sony Pictures Animation, Inc. All rights reserved.

Printed in the United States of America.

For information address HarperCollins Children's Books, a division of HarperCollins Publishers, 1350 Avenue of the Americas, New
York, NY 10019.

www.icanread.com

Library of Congress catalog card number: 2007921503

ISBN-13: 978-0-06-115327-3 — ISBN-10: 0-06-115327-3

❖

First Edition

SURF'S UP™
ISLAND ADVENTURES

Adapted by Lisa Rao

HarperCollins*Publishers*

Cody Maverick loved to surf.

He even made his own surfboard.

He carved it out of a block of ice.

Cody dreamed of going to Pen Gu Island,

where it was warm and

he could surf all day long.

The other penguins

thought Cody was nuts.

Even his brother, Glen, told him that

penguins don't surf.

Glen thought Cody should quit dreaming.

But Cody had other plans.

One morning, Cody saw a whale.

The whale was going to Pen Gu Island!

"I've got to catch that whale!"

Cody thought.

The whale was going fast.

But Cody had his ice-board.

He could go faster.

He sliced through the water.

He caught up with the whale.

Chicken Joe helped him aboard.

"Hi! I'm a surfer, too," Chicken Joe said.
"My name is Joseph. It's long for Joe.
You are the best surfer I've ever seen.
Is that surfboard made of ice? Cool!"
"Thanks for helping me," Cody said.
"It was my pleasure," replied Joe.

"I never saw anyone rip up a wave like that!"

Cody and Joe became best buddies.

The whale finally arrived at Pen Gu.

"This place is great," said Cody.

"It's even better than I imagined!"

Joe ran off to buy some food.

"Hey, Cody! Try this," said Joe.

"What is it?" Cody asked.

"It's squid on a stick," said Joe.

"Take a bite! You'll love it."

Cody thought it tasted like chicken!

But he didn't tell that to Chicken Joe.

"Hmm. It's not bad," Cody said.

Cody and Joe watched a lifeguard running into the water.

"She's beautiful!" Cody said to Joe.

"I wonder who she is."

Lani the lifeguard stared back at Cody.

Joe laughed. "She likes you, too, dude!"

Lani turned quickly and kept running.

Lani raced to the water.

"Come on, little guy," she said.

"You'll be fine."

Cody was impressed.

"That was great," said Cody.

"I'm Cody."

"My name is Lani. Are you new here?"
Lani asked.

"Just arrived from Shiverpool,"
Cody answered.

"I can't wait to hit the waves."

Lani took Cody on a tour of the island.

"These are lava tubes," Lani said.

"Come on!"

"This is great!" Cody said.

"It's like a slide in the dark."

"Watch out for the green pool!"
Lani laughed.

"Why?" asked Cody. "It's cool!
It's bubbly and glows in the dark!"

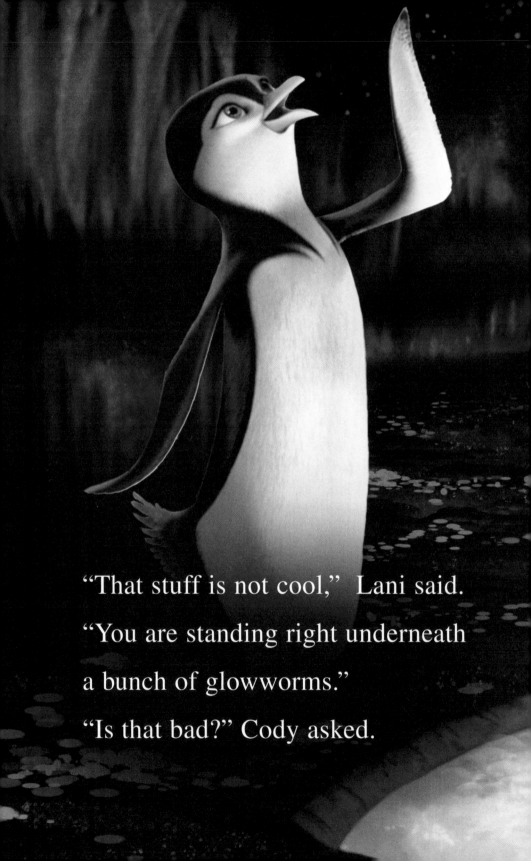

"That stuff is not cool," Lani said.
"You are standing right underneath
a bunch of glowworms."
"Is that bad?" Cody asked.

"Well, that depends." Lani said.
"Do you like being covered
in glowworm poop?"

"Ugh! I'm covered in poop!"

yelled Cody.

Lani held her breath.

"What's the matter?" Cody asked her.

"Cody! You stink!" she said.

Cody took a long time

scrubbing glowworm poop

off of his feathers.

While Cody got himself cleaned up,

Joe went looking for his buddy.

He found some island natives instead.

They tied Joe to a long pole

and carried him to a big pot of hot water.

"Wow, a hot tub!" said Joe.

"Are you guys coming in, too? No?

You mean this is all for me? Cool!"

The natives danced around the pot.

The natives added vegetables to the pot.

Joe said, "A free meal, too? Wow!

But I have to find my buddy, Cody."

Joe climbed out of the pot.

"Thanks, guys!

Let's do this again," he said.

The natives were surprised.

They ran after Joe.

Joe thought the natives looked hungry.

He handed them some squid on a stick.

The natives loved it!

Then the natives talked to each other
in a language Joe couldn't understand.
The natives were saying,
"This tastes like chicken!"

Joe finally found Cody and Lani.

"Cody! My main man!" Joe said.

"I've been looking all over for you.

I see you have company.

If you'd rather be alone . . ."

Joe smiled at Lani.

Cody blushed and grabbed Joe.

"Hey, check out the surf," Cody said.

"What time is it, dudes?" Joe asked.

"Time to hit the waves!" Lani shouted.

Cody, Joe, and Lani shouted to each other in the water.

"This is awesome!" they yelled.

And the three new best friends surfed together until the sun went down.